BILLY DON'T BE A BULLY

By Sherelyn Duhart

*This book is dedicated to bullies and those who are
or have been bullied. As you read, please realize
bullies come in all age groups, races, both genders,
and they can live anywhere in the world.
I truly believe you will be inspired.
I dedicate this book to you with love,
that is unconditional love.*

BILLY DON'T BE A BULLY

Bullying is not right. It is not kind. Bullying is a very aggressive act. I cannot stand to see someone bullied, physically or verbally abused. I despise both. I believe adults and children can glean from this book. It is a great family book which can lead to all types of discussions. This is a revised edition. A second edition with a workbook. I hope it inspires you to want to act.

Duhart Press LLC www.duhartpress.com Printed in USA

Contact author for speaking engagements at sduhart1@yahoo,com or sduhart1@bellsouth.net. Fb:Sherelyn Duhart IG: sherelynduhart

Books can be purchased as paperbacks or ebooks on Kindle, Amazon, Barnes & Noble, Walmart.com, Kobo, Tolino, 24 Symbols, Barnes & Taylor, Overdrive, Apple, Playster, Scribd, and Bibliotheca.

Contents

<u>The Neighborhood</u>

Once upon a time there was a child named Billy Williams.
Billy was the bully in the Greenwich community. Billy is a
miserable young man. He moved to Greenwich from
Houston with his parents. His mom and dad do not spend
any time with him at all. His father works long hours every
day, his mother works two jobs, and she is a member of
several organizations.

Michael and Gerald are close friends who also live in Greenwich. Veronica is Michael's sister; she is in high school and volunteers at the hospital. Michael and Veronica have the perfect family—at least that is what everyone in the neighborhood thinks. Their parents are loving and attentive to their children. They spend quality time with them.

James lives in the community; he is great at karate, but he does not flaunt his karate skills and rarely uses them. James's parents spend a lot of time with him. His parents were born in Japan, but he was born in America.

Abdul lives there also, he is of Indian descent. He's a cool guy. He does not wear his Indian garb all the time. He does wear his head wrap to the swimming pool. His parents wear their Indian attire almost every day.

Juanita and Ellen are sisters; they are one year apart and like to play together. They are very pretty girls with long hair. Their parents are both doctors. They have a good relationship with their parents.

All the children in this community attend the same school and the same church. Billy has noticed how the children in the neighborhood interact with their parents. Michael, James, and Abdul spend time with their parents. James is always outside talking to his father. Michael and his father play catch together at least once or twice a week. Abdul plays basketball with his dad.

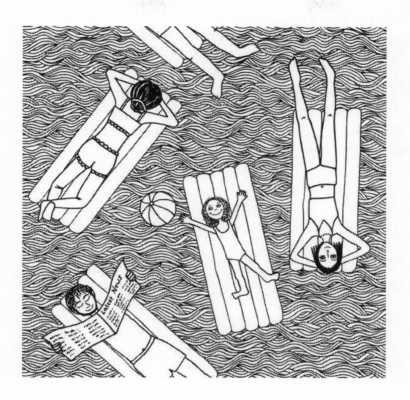

The Hot Spot -The Swimming Pool

The children are at the community swimming pool; this is their favorite place to hang out. School is out, and they're excited because this is the first week of their vacation. It is a hot summer day in June, and everyone is having a great time. Billy is about to bother Juanita and Ellen, he wants to pull their hair and harass them.

"Ouch!" yelled Juanita. "Stop it. Don't pull my hair!"

3

Billy ran away and got a drink in the snack area. He returned shoving the girls as he passed by them.

"Stop pushing me!" yelled Ellen.

"Stop!" yelled Juanita.

Billy gave the girls such a hard push that they fell. The girls helped each other up; they were angry with Billy.

"What a bully!" screamed Juanita.

"He needs to pick on someone his own size!" yelled Ellen.

The girls decided to go home. Billy's mother was turning in her driveway as they passed her home.

"Hello!" said Juanita and Ellen.

"Hello!" responded Mrs. Williams.

"How are you doing today?" asked Juanita.

"I'm okay. I had a rough, and busy day, which is why I am home early!" responded Mrs. Williams.

"Sorry to hear that, Mrs. Williams. This might not be a good time to bring this up, but Billy is bothering us. We cannot go to the swimming pool in peace!" stated Ellen.

"Mrs. Williams, we left the swimming pool early because Billy pushed us down and pulled our hair. We don't like telling on him, but we know if we don't say something, his bad behavior will continue. We had the same type of experience last year with a guy in school. He kept bullying

4

us. We learned that we should speak up. Billy is getting on my nerves. Will you tell him to stop?" asked Juanita.

"He has been doing what? He knows better! He knows he is not supposed to touch girls or ladies. His father has taught him better! Wait until I tell his father! I apologize for my son's behavior!" said Mrs. Williams.

"Thanks, Mrs. Williams. I feel kind of bad about snitching on him. I do know he will continue if we don't speak up!" responded Juanita.

"You are welcome. Billy knows I don't have time for any nonsense. I am too busy to be bothered with foolishness," stated Mrs. Williams.

Juanita and Ellen were relieved they'd had a chance to talk with Billy's mother. They both felt like a load had been lifted from their shoulders. The girls wondered what she would say to Billy. They wished they could be flies on the wall.

"Mom, I'm home! You are home early, Mom!" screamed Billy.

"Billy, why did you push the girls next door? And you pulled their hair. You are always bothering someone. What do we have to do to control your behavior? I don't have time to be bothered with foolishness. Leave the girls next door alone! You know your dad and I do not tolerate that kind of behavior. You are supposed to treat girls like princesses!" shouted his mom.

"They are exaggerating. I did not push them down." replied Billy.

5

"I can tell when you are not telling the truth." said his mom.

"Don't do it again!"

"Okay, Mom! I will not go near them!" yelled Billy. *I wish I could hit those girls for snitching on me, he thought. That is against the code for our age group. I had better not bother them, or my parents will rip me to shreds. My parents only pay attention to me when I get in trouble. Otherwise they just ignore me. I wish my parents spent time with me. The other children in the neighborhood get to spend time with their parents.*

The next day, Reggie and Abdul were at the pool having a great time. The heat from the sun is scorching. Getting in the pool cools them off every time they jump in the pool.

"Hey, Reggie! Aren't you glad school is out? Where is James? I just knew he would be here?" inquired Abdul.

"What's up? You know I am glad school is out." replied Reggie.

"Man, you know James takes karate lessons during the summer—swimming is secondary for him, and karate is first. He is about to become a black belt."

"That's right, I forgot. Last one in the pool is a rotten egg!" yelled Abdul. "I will beat you!" screamed Reggie.

Abdul and Reggie are racing to the pool. This event is an everyday thing. It is very challenging to the both of them. It is a part of their daily fun.

"I won!" yelled Abdul.

"I let you have that." stated Reggie.

"You know I beat you! I win every day. Reggie this water feels good. It is hot today! I could stay in the water all day!" yelled Abdul.

"It's cooling me off!" responded Reggie.

Billy sees Reggie and Abdul and is anxiously awaiting to bully them. He is like an animal looking for prey. He is looking for someone to pick on.

"What's that thing on your head?" asked Billy as he passed by Reggie and Abdul.

Billy noticed that Abdul was turning red. *He's not happy I'm bothering him, and I can tell he wants me to leave him alone, thought Billy.* "It looks like a mop."

Abdul turned around and looked at Billy. He did not say a mumbling word, but his feelings were hurt.

"Who is that?" asked Reggie.

"He is that new kid that moved here from Houston. I have heard he is trouble," said Abdul. "That guy is trying to spoil all my fun. I don't want to be bothered with him, but I don't know how to respond. If he would just go away, everything would be all right."

"Oh yeah! I heard someone talking about him the other day. I heard them say he is a menace." replied Reggie.

Billy snatches Abdul's wrap off his head. Abdul is not happy about this. As a matter of fact, he is angry. On the other hand, Billy is gloating and laughing. Abdul thinks

Billy is obnoxious and a creep. Of course, he does not say this out loud.

"Give it back! Give it back!" yelled Abdul. *Oh crap. What am I going to do? My heart is skipping a beat. I wish I could blink, and he would be gone.* "Just leave us alone!"

"Come and get it!" screamed Billy. "Come and get it! Come and get it!" *He is an easy target, thought Billy. I know I am getting under his skin. I will keep aggravating him. He is getting madder as I get further and further away.* "Ha! Ha! Ha!"

"Bring it back!" screamed Abdul.

"He's gone! Some nerve!" stated Reggie as he and Abdul got out of the pool.

"Are you ready to go?" asked Abdul. "I am so upset. I have never been so humiliated or felt so useless."

"Yes! I hear you Abdul. He is a trip," replied Reggie.

"See you tomorrow!" stated Abdul. *Billy has ruined my day. I hope this is not an indication of what my summer is going to be like.*

"Maybe we should go to the pool at an earlier time. We go at 2 pm every day, maybe we should go before 12 noon. Hopefully, we will not see this Billy boy". stated Abdul.

"We should smack him upside the head, but he runs away so fast we cannot get to him. One minute he is there, and the next, he's gone. We should jump him," said Reggie.

8

"I don't want to go to the pool anymore if he comes. You never know what he might come up with!" said Abdul. "Out of the blue Billy seems to have decided to bother me."

The boys go to the pool a couple hours earlier the next day.

"It's another hot one!" stated Abdul. "I can't wait to enjoy the water today. I hope we have no interruptions. It would be nice to get some laps in."

"It's ninety-five degrees today, but the water feels so good," stated Reggie. "Come on and get in, Abdul! I hope that Billy does not come today. We need to enjoy the water as long as we can."

"Watch out! Here I come! Oh yes! It feels good!" yelled Abdul.

"I will race you from one end of the pool to the other! Get in position. Are you ready?" asked Reggie.

"Yeah!" replied Abdul.

"On your mark, get set, ready, go!" yelled Reggie.

The boys took off swimming across the pool at top speed.

"I won! I won!" said Abdul as he touched the side of the pool first.

"Both of you are sorry! I can beat both of you!" said Billy as he drew closer to Abdul. *I am going to really make him mad today. Watch out here I come.*

Billy swam over to Abdul and grabbed his headgear. Laughing, Billy held it above his head.

"Give it here!" yelled Abdul. "Give it here!" *He is getting on my nerves. I am tired of him taken off my headgear.*

"You can have it if you can catch me!" yelled Billy.

With that, he left the swimming pool and ran toward home. *I know I am irritating him.*

"That Billy boy has taken my headgear twice! I am tired of him. Reggie let's find some other place to hang out." said Abdul. "I am furious."

"I hear you. I am tired of him too. I will ask my cousin down the street if we can swim in his pool. I would like to swim in peace. I will call him as soon as I get in the house!" stated Reggie. *I hate that Abdul is having this problem with Billy, but to be honest, I am glad it is not me.*

10

Michael Meets Billy

The next day Reggie and Abdul were swimming at Reggie's cousin's pool. They were happy because now there wouldn't be any Billy problems.

The swimming pool was crowded with kids having fun; Billy was looking for a new target, since Abdul and Reggie were nowhere to be found. Billy spotted Michael having a good time and decided to bother him.

"This lemonade is good!" said Gerald as he gulped it down. "It sure is refreshing."
"It is cooling me off in this heat and quenching my thirst," exclaimed Michael.

"I bet you I can drink mine more quickly than you can drink yours," said Gerald.

"No way! I will beat you. You know I beat you at everything," replied Michael. *Gerald is sorry at everything compared to me. I always beat him, no matter what we're doing.*

Billy walked up and knocked the lemonade out of Michael's hand.
"Oh, my!" yelled Michael with disgust as he looked at his lemonade sliding down his body. *Who is this guy? This has got to be that Billy boy everyone is talking about.*

Billy stated, "What are you going to do scary-cat?" *Look at his face—he looks like he saw a ghost.*

Michael did not say anything; he just held his head down in disgust. He wanted to retaliate, but he was afraid.

"What are you going to do?" Billy yelled. *I know I have him right where I want him. SCARED!* "Michael is a scary-cat, Michael is a scary-cat!"

"Why didn't you say something? I would love to, but he is not bothering me," said Gerald. *Mike is getting on my nerves because he will not speak up.*

"Look, Gerald, I hate to admit it, but I am scared. The words would not come out. I know if I don't speak up, the bullying will more than likely continue. I feel bad about not saying anything," stated Michael. *Billy is twice as tall and big as me. He looks like a giant.*

"Are you ready to go? That Billy has spoiled all the fun!" said Gerald with obvious disappointment. "I guess I understand you not wanting to fight him. He looks like a giant compared to us."

"He is rather big and tall! See you tomorrow," said Michael."Yes, tomorrow. I hope we don't run into Billy. He is a terror," said Gerald. *Michael probably needs to get an adult to intervene on his behalf. I know that is out of the question. He likes to hide things from his parents.*

Michael entered his house and moved toward the kitchen.

"Michael is that you?" his mother asks. "You are home early from the swimming pool. Is everything okay?"

"Yes, Mom, everything is okay. I just came back early." said Michael. *I know my mom would have a fit if she found out I am lying to her. She knows me like a book. She really pays attention to us. She realizes I am home early. There is no fooling her. She can keep asking questions, but I am not going to tell her yet*

"Okay, dinner will be ready in an hour," his mom responds.

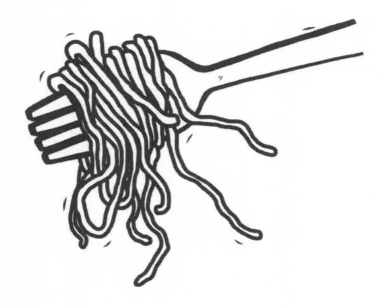

It's All in the Family

Michael has a mom who pays attention to him, shows him love, and is concerned about his well-being. His mother and his father build him up and encourage him. Michael makes straight A's in school. His father plays sports with him and spends quality time with him. The family is the ideal family God has created. It's dinnertime at Michael's house, and the family is gathered around the table.

14

"Dear heavenly Father, thank you for this food we are about to receive. Let it nourish our bodies, in Jesus' name," prayed Michael's father.

Everyone agreed with the prayer by saying "Amen."

"Honey, how was your day? Did you finish that manuscript you were working on?" asked dad.

Excited about her accomplishment Michael's mom answered, "Yes, I did. I barely made it. It looks like the book will be ready for printing within the next thirty days. Thanks for asking."

Dad turned to Veronica next and asked, "Princess, how was your day?"

"Dad, my day was awesome," Veronica answered. "I watched the nurses as they assisted several patients. It can be gross at times, especially when I see the bloody victims."

"You see blood?" asked Mom." Oh my, I don't know if you should see all of that. I believe you are too young to see some of the things you see at the hospital."

"Honey, I understand what you are saying," said Dad. "Veronica, I must admit I am not excited about you seeing some of the patients. We do have to trust God. You are thinking about becoming a doctor, and I hope this will help you decide if this path is for you. We will support the desires that God has placed on your heart and his purpose for your life. We will do everything we need to do for you to reach your short-term goals and your long-term goals. I know seeing blood is part of the job, but honestly, I think you don't have to see blood to make a decision. I think you might need to back off on the trauma and blood cases."

" Dad! I did volunteer, and they told me I did not have to be involved in the more serious cases," responded Veronica.

"I am glad you understand," responded her father.

"By the way, honey, you really prepared a good meal tonight. Now, Michael, it is your turn—how was your day?"

"It was great!" said Michael smiling. *I am lying through my pearly whites. I hope my family cannot tell. I am not ready to tell them. I am nervous, because my parents can always tell when I am lying.*

Dad looked at mom with a puzzled look. Then he said, "Michael, you usually have more to say than it was great. Are you sure your day was great?"

"Yes, Dad, it was great," said Michael. *Another lie. They are adding up.*

"All right, Mike. You know if you are lying, we will find out the truth," stated his mom.

"Everything that is hidden shall be revealed. Guess, what I did today?" asked his dad.

Everyone asked excitedly, "What?"

"I paid the balance on our vacation to Disney World! We have forty-five days until vacation. I am excited and I hope you all are too. I could use a vacation." said Dad.

"Dad, I am excited! Disney is one place I am not tired of," said Veronica.

"I'm excited, too! I am ready for a vacation!" screamed Michael.

"I think we all could use a vacation," their father responded.

"Yes, we could." replied their mother.

"I am ready!" responded Veronica.

What Should We Do?

"Man, my dad is taking us on vacation to Disney World in August, and I cannot wait," said Michael. "I hope Billy will have stopped bullying me by the time I go on vacation. It is getting old fast."

"That is great. We are going to Panama City. Disney World is always fun!" said Gerald. "Do you want to go to the swimming pool?"

"Yes! I hope Billy does not come today. I am scared. I don't know what I did to make him want to pick on me all the time," said Michael, looking confused. *I don't want anyone to know how scared I really am. No one has any idea.*

"We don't want Billy to stop us from going to the pool. Even though you are afraid of him. You cannot show him that you are scared," said Gerald.

"You are right, but Lord knows my knees shake and my heart skips several beats when I see him," explained Michael. "This fear has me reading my Bible more."

"Let's go! Mike. For your sake, I hope he is not there," said Gerald.

The boys are on their way to the pool. As they approach the pool, Michael sees Billy standing near the entrance.

"Oh, my goodness! Billy is waiting on us at the door!" said Michael nervously.

"Why is he here so early? I was hoping that Billy wouldn't be here this early." said Gerald. We have to do something about this because I am tired of him bothering you."

"We have to go in! We cannot act like wimps," said Michael. *I feel like a wimp on the inside. I feel useless. Why me? I did not do anything. I need to tell my parents or someone, but I don't know how.*

"What's taking you so long to come to the pool?" Billy asked. "You're scared of me—I know you are. I am not going to bother you yet. I might let you swim a little bit before I bother you." *I cannot wait to get my hands on him.*

*He thinks he is something with that big house and a
Mercedes. Well, just because his dad plays ball with him
does not make him better than me. He is full of himself. I
will get him. I cannot stand the ground he walks on.*

As Gerald and Michael walk into the pool area, Billy shoves
Michael into the wall.

"How do you like that? Most people would push me back—
what are you going to do, scary-cat?" yelled Billy.

"Please don't push me!" yelled Michael. *I cannot believe I
said that. I am proud of myself. Lord help me. Billy is
getting on my nerves, Lord.*

"You don't tell me what to do. I will push you again!" said
Billy. *This Michael has a lot of nerves. He is trying to get an
attitude. I know he is scared because when he sees me his
eyes get big.* "Are you scared? Why don't you fight me,
Michael? Why are you running? Push me or something!"
yelled Billy.

"I gotta go!" yelled Michael as he ran away.

"Chicken! Scary-cat!" yelled Billy. *I am getting the best of
him. I have him running. This is good.*

Michael ran home and dashed into the house, slamming the
door behind him. He was breathing hard and heavy.
Veronica was in the house and looked up from her book
with concern. She asks her brother in a concerned way.

20

"Are you okay, Michael? You're slamming doors, and it sounds like you're out of breath?" asked Veronica.

"I'm fine. I appreciate your concern Sis." Michael replies. *I have lied again. I just ran from Billy, and I know that was the wrong thing to do. He probably knows for sure he has the upper hand, and I am scared out of my wits. I know I must do something.*

"I am glad you are okay—you scared me running in here as if you were being chased by a wild animal!" said Veronica. *I know he is lying to me. I am going to play along with him and see how long he keeps telling me lies*

"Veronica are you going to Vacation Bible School?" asked Michael. *I know I must change the subject fast or she will figure out I am lying to her. My sister is very smart and discerning.*

"I plan to. I might not make it every day, but I know I will make it at least one day." responded Veronica.

"Well, it starts tomorrow morning, so you might want to make up your mind," said Michael. "I am going every day. I will be there first thing tomorrow."

"Great! I will try to be there, too," said Veronica. "I had better get to bed because tomorrow morning will be here before you know it." *I noticed how my brother changed the subject. I am tired. Sooner or later whatever he is hiding will come to light.*

It's the next morning, Michael is up bright and early. He is excited about getting a break from Billy. He is ready to try something new and that is Vacation Bible School.

"Good morning everyone. I am off to Vacation Bible School. I believe it is over by noon," stated Michael.

"I am ecstatic that you are going to Vacation Bible School, but I am surprised because you usually prefer swimming. You are acting a little strange, Mike. Why the sudden change?" asked his mom.

"Mom, people change. I decided to listen to what you and dad have been telling me. You told me I needed to seek the Lord more. That is why I have decided to go to

Vacation Bible School. There will still be time to go to the pool," stated Michael.

"Okay! Whatever you say, but it is a little strange," responded Mom. *Something is going on in my son's life. I will find out sooner or later.*

"Gotta go! Later!" yelled Michael.

Well, here I am on my way to Vacation Bible School. I am excited about going because I need some answers. I walk in and to my amazement there are a lot of kids my age there. I am surprised; they are alert and up at nine o'clock in the morning. I am a little late. I am so amazed at the topic of the lessons for the week. One is love your enemies, Walk in forgiveness toward bullies, classmates, etc. Can you believe that they are talking about praying for those who treat you badly or spitefully? I am getting insight as to why Billy is bullying me. The teachers have been talking about how he might not be happy with his life. And he might want to make everyone else unhappy like he is.

I am so thankful for Vacation Bible School. I am learning a lot about how to treat people. Wow, I am learning that love covers a multitude of sins. God is saying I must love this Billy even when he mistreats me. At the same time, the teachers say that if a bully bothers you, you must tell someone. The bullying will never stop if someone in authority does not step in. Oh my. I must tell someone what is going on. I have not been to the swimming pool this week. I am getting so much information and learning so much. I am just thinking and thanking God for helping me with my problem. Even after I have received all this word. I am still scared. I need God to help me get over the fear of confronting Billy. It has been a week since I have gone swimming. Lord knows I want to go back to the pool. Gerald keeps asking me questions. He knows why I might not want to go to the swimming pool. He knows I like to swim and cannot believe I have missed five days at the swimming pool. Today is Friday. I think I am going to meet Gerald at the swimming pool tomorrow.

"Hey, Mike!" said Gerald. "It's about time you showed up. You have been missing in action. Billy has been looking crazy. He looks lost without you to pick on."

"Gerald, I have not missed him. I have had a peaceful week without being bullied by him." said Michael. "It would be nice to enjoy today at the swimming pool without being bothered with Billy."

23

"I don't think he is coming today Mike. He has not seen you all week. I think you are safe. Let's enjoy a nice peaceful swim," said Gerald. "Check it out—we have been here for about an hour and still no Billy. He usually shows up by now."

"Yeah, Gerald you are right!" said Michael. *I have decided to calm down. Time is ticking away. We are having a peaceful time at the pool. I thank God for this time. Wow, I am swimming laps around the pool how refreshing. Oh, thank you Lord, for an awesome time at the pool today. I am going home smiling.*

"Our swim time was awesome. Mike, see you tomorrow." said Gerald.

"Okay, later gator!" said Michael. *I think I will take a shower and go to bed early. I am so relaxed from my swimming. Thank you, Lord, for letting me have a pleasant time at the swimming pool. Maybe Billy will not be at the pool anymore. I cannot wait to go tomorrow.*

"Mike, did you have a good time at the swimming pool?" asked his mom.

"Yes, Mother I did. I just finished taking my shower. I am so relaxed. I am going to bed early I am so excited about the peaceful time I had today at the pool." replied Mike.

"Honey, I am glad your swim time was very relaxing. Don't spend all your time at the pool. Did you enjoy Vacation Bible School?" asked his mom.

"It was very interesting, Mom. I learned about forgiveness and love," said Michael.

"Forgiveness and love are two powerful topics. Love is one of the ten commandments God gave us. And God wants us to forgive our brothers and sisters if we want him to forgive us. So, does this mean you are going to be at church more often now?" asked his mom.

"I think so, Mom. I really enjoyed it and can understand it," replied Michael. *I am glad mom is happy with my life. I am happy, too. I have a strange feeling I will face Billy again. I will be concerned about that tomorrow. Right now, I am going to bed and savor the moments.*

"Good morning, Mike. Mom was telling me you had a great time at the swimming pool yesterday. She also said you plan to go to church more often. I can't believe it. That is awesome," said Veronica.

"Yeah Veronica, it is true. My time at the pool was awesome. I was inspired and thankful when God answered my prayer today. And Vacation Bible School was good." said Michael.

"Good my brother! What are you getting ready to do?" asked Veronica.

"I am getting ready to go the swimming pool. I am meeting Gerald over there." responded Mike. *I hope my time at the swimming pool is peaceful.*

"Hey, Mike!" yelled Gerald.

25

"What's up?" responded Mike. "Hey, last one in the pool hates his mom."

"I won!" yelled Gerald.

"No man, you know I won!" said Mike. "Oh, man here he comes. It's like he is watching our every move." *I hope he does not get in. That was wishful thinking—here comes Billy.*

Billy dives in the pool and swims toward Michael.

Oh, no, it looks like he's headed my way. Wait a minute, where'd he go? "That big head Billy has hit me in my back. I can't move. Oh, it hurts!" yelled Mike."

"Mike are you okay? I saw what he did! How does your back feel? The color has changed!" yelled Gerald.

"Gerald, man, it hurts. I cannot move. Come help me. I can't go home. I can't let my family see me bent over. Do you think I can go over to your house? He hit me hard, and I would hit him, even though I'm scared, but he's always running away." screamed Michael.

"It's cool, my friend you can come over. I know we have a heating pad, and probably some Ben-gay. Maybe you can take some pain pills. That is what my parents do when they are hurting." replied Gerald with much dismay.

"Help me out the pool!" said Michael.

"Okay!" replied Gerald. *I am tired of Billy. Mike must do something. There have been a lot of incidents involving bullies. There was an incident where one bully kept bothering a boy and that boy hurt himself. He did damage to himself because he did not know why he was being bullied. There was another instance where some girls were bothering one girl, and she did something crazy. I cannot remember what it was. I need to help him, but I don't know what to do. I think I am going to tell someone in authority— maybe his parents or maybe his sister.*

"Thanks, Gerald. Are you okay? You seem to be in deep thought. It is okay if I come over your house?" asked Mike.

"Of course, Mike. It is okay. I was just thinking about this bullying, man. Something must be done. Hold on, Mike, we are almost there," responded Gerald.

"Thanks, Gerald. Yes, something must be done. I know I need to do something fast. I will figure it out soon." *I still don't know why he chose me to pick on. I remember that I learned in Vacation Bible School that everyone needs love. I guess Billy needs love. He sure is hard to love. Just because he needs love and attention does not give him the right to make me his punching bag. I have four days before my vacation. Maybe I will figure it out before or during my vacation.*

"Mike, just rest here for two to three hours then you go home. Take a shower, too. While you rest, we can watch that new movie that is out." stated Gerald.

"Okay, sounds good." replied Mike.

27

The boys watched the movie, and as time passed, Mike's back began to feel better.

"I hope my back heals fast. I hope the color on my back comes back, it is black and blue. Billy hit me hard." said Mike. *Gerald gives me some clothes to wear while I rest and wait for my back to get better. Gerald is right—something must be done. Oh, Lord, what I am going to do?* "Well, Gerald, I had better go. Thanks for everything. Is my back getting back to its normal color?" said Mike.

"Mike, you are welcome. You know you are my boy. And the color on your back is coming back. I think you should stay away from the swimming pool, at least one day." said Gerald.

"I think I will. Thanks again," said Mike.

"Later!" said Gerald.

Swimming Pool Saga

"Mike is that you?" asked Veronica.

"Yes, sis! It's me," replied Mike.

"Juanita called! Then Ellen called! They did not leave specific messages," called Veronica.

"Okay! Thanks! I am going to my room to rest," said Mike.

"Cool!" replied Veronica.

"Later! See you at dinner," replied Mike." I think I will take a nap first, and when I wake up I will call the girls."

My nap was good. I will call Juanita's cell phone first. She is not answering. I will leave a message. Now, I'll call Ellen.

"Hello?" said Ellen.

"Hey, Ellen! You called?" asked Mike.

29

"Yes, I did. We heard what happened at the swimming pool. And we also heard this was not the first time," stated Ellen.

"Word sure gets around fast! There are no secrets in our community," replied Mike.

"Mike, did you know that he pulled Juanita's hair and mine. He pushed us also. We were scared. We told on him. We had to get over the fact that everyone might call us a snitch. There have been too many horror stories about people getting bullied. We told his mother, and he has not bothered us since. Billy lives next door to us, so you can imagine, we are somewhat still nervous," stated Ellen.

"You did? And he has not bothered you since? That is good. It's okay for a girl to snitch. Guys look like a wimp, if we do it. I know I have to do something," replied Michael.

"Look, Mike, I have known you since the first grade. I would hate for something to happen to you. You are like a brother to me," explained Ellen.

"I know, Ellen! I don't want anything to happen to me either. Believe me—I am going to do something. I hope and pray that I don't wait too late. Thanks for your concern," replied Mike.

"You are welcome. I just don't want anything to happen to you. I hope I don't sound like a robot, by repeating the same thing," said Ellen.

"Okay thanks for your concern. It's time for dinner, Ellen. My mother and father love for us to eat together. Please tell

Juanita thanks. Love you," said Mike. *It's dinnertime at my house. I truly hope no one in my family has heard about the swimming pool incident. The food smells good. I love eating with my family, but sometimes I hate it because my family picks up on things.*

"Honey, it was hot today. I wish I could go to the swimming pool like Mike. You will not catch me in a bikini any time soon. I have to lose some of this weight," said Michael's mom.

"Ah, Mom, you look good. You are always tripping about your weight. My classmates are always bragging about how good and how young you look," said Veronica. "Did you hear about the bully at the swimming pool? Mike have you ran into him? I heard he has picked on some girls, and he has been picking on some guys. He is a terror. From my understanding the girls told his mother. Some of the children have stopped going to the pool. And he is still bothering some guys! He is a trip!"

"Bullies are cowards. Most of the time, they are having some problem at home and need love," said their dad.

"Yes, they are. They have been around a long time. God bless them. From my understanding they have a low self-esteem, also," said mom.

"Yes, they are very unhappy people. Mike have you seen the bully?" asked Veronica again.

"No, I have not," responded Mike. "You know the swimming pool area is very big. It could have taken place anywhere."

"I am surprised you have not heard. You know how people talk," responded Veronica. *Mike has heard about Billy the bully. He just does not want to tell me. I will find out soon. He cannot hide it from me.*

"That is good, Mike. You don't know anything about it. I hope the victim does not hold it in. I hope he or she lets someone know what is going on. I know people don't like to snitch," said his mom.

"Bullies never pick on someone their own size," stated Veronica.

"Enough of that! Dad how much money will you give us to spend while we are on vacation?" asked Mike. *I decided to change the subject. I hope it was not too noticeable. Our vacation is only three days away.*

"Dad, how much are you going to give us?" asked Veronica. *I am aware my brother has changed the subject. It was smooth the way he did it—picking a topic that everyone is excited about.*

"Before I give you any money, you must spend fifty dollars of your allowance. I want you to budget how much money you are going to spend. Do not always expect me to pay for things, when I give you money twice a month," answered their father.

"Your father is right. You must spend your money, and budget it appropriately," said Michael's mom.

"Ah, mom, ah dad, that is not fair," responded Mike.

"Yeah, Mom, and Dad, you are being hard. Come on, please give us some money. I don't want to spend my money. Oh Daddy!" said Veronica.

"My dear, children, I have spoken. Now work with what you have. I have paid for your tickets to the park. I paid for the hotel. I will more than likely pay for your breakfast, lunch, and dinner. What more can you ask? Anything else you want on the trip comes out of your pocket," said their father. "Honey, before I get up from the table, I want you to know the food was good." said the father.

"Thanks, honey. I hope everyone enjoyed the dinner," said his mom.

"I did! May I be excused?" said Veronica.

"Yes, you may!" replied Dad. "And you may leave, too, Mike."

"Thanks, Veronica. I am glad you enjoyed the food," said their mom.

"Mom, I enjoyed the food, also. Thanks, Dad for excusing me. I love you, family. I am going upstairs to research some things. I might see you all later in the den, especially if a good movie comes on. I think might start packing tonight, also," said Mike. *That Veronica knows something. She was probing. And my silly butt wants to go to the swimming pool again. I had better start packing. I am excited about getting away.*

"Mike, telephone!" called Mom.

"Okay! I got it! Hello?" said Michael.

"Hey, Mike, I was just thinking. I think we should hold off on going to the swimming pool," said Gerald. "At least until after school starts."

"You know, Gerald, you are probably right! I know I am playing on dangerous ground. I know I should avoid Billy and tell on him. I do know that I am not going to allow him to hurt me seriously. I might be scared, but I love myself. See you tomorrow," said Mike.

"Okay, partner. Whatever you say. Just thinking about your own good. See you tomorrow," said Gerald.

With only three days before his family's summer vacation Mike is in a great mood. The temperature is in the low 90s. Mike and Gerald decided to take their chances, it is too hot not to get in that pool. They know that the word of God says fear not for I am with thee. They also know they are supposed to report Billy.

Michael and Gerald were standing near the pool's edge when they spotted Billy; all the children looked on. Billy is heading their way, you have to know he might be up to something. Billy pushed Michael into the pool, causing a big splash that hit Gerald.

34

"You are going to get it one day, you big bully. You are nothing but a coward, pushing my friend in and then you run. Only a coward runs!" yelled Gerald.

The lifeguard dove in to make sure Michael was okay. The lifeguard was furious and made an announcement to the children that there should be no horseplay in or around the pool.

"Who pushed you?" asked the lifeguard. Michael was silent, and no one said anything.

"You mean to tell me that no one knows who this guy is?" asked the lifeguard.

"No, we don't know him, answered Mike. "It all happened so fast." *I am becoming a big liar. I have told so many lies lately.*

"I have to file a report. If anyone knows who this person is. Please come see me or call me. You can remain anonymous," said the lifeguard.

"We will when we find out who this person is," said Gerald.

"We sure will," replied Mike. "Thanks for all your help."

"You are welcome," replied the lifeguard.

"Let's get out of here. Mike, we will not come here for the rest of the summer. I told you we should not come to the pool today," stated Gerald.

"Yes, you told me, and I should have listened. But I wanted to be bullheaded. Now the lifeguard must file a report. Veronica is going to hear about this," responded Michael. *I will finish packing and act like I am so excited about the vacation. I will pretend to be sick. Tomorrow will be two days before vacation.*

"See you later, Mike! You are going to have to tell someone soon. If something else happens, and I am standing right there, I will tell for you. You had better hope the lifeguard does not tell," said Gerald.

"Okay, later. Yes, I hope he does not tell my parents," said Mike. *I will go home and start, or shall I say finish packing. I don't believe that Billy pushed me in the water. I am so tired of him. He is a true menace. I remember another scripture from Vacation Bible School—you shall reap what you sow Billy is going to reap all that he has done to people. I have done some packing. It's about midnight. I will watch a movie, so I can sleep late in the morning. When I wake up, I can make sure all my clothes are clean.*

Michael doesn't wake up until almost 2:00 p.m. He had messages from his friends who had called while he was still asleep.

"What time did you go to bed last night? You must be tired. I have been calling you all morning," Veronica asked.

"Okay, Veronica. I must have been tired. I went to bed after one o'clock. I will call all of them back today or tomorrow," responded Mike.

"They all asked that you call them back as soon as possible," said Veronica.

"Okay, by the time I take my shower it will be almost three o'clock." said Michael. *I am going to take my shower, get a quick bite to eat and then start making my calls. I have an idea what they want to talk about. I am going to wash a couple of loads, so that I can have some clean clothes for the vacation. I had better start calling my friends. I will call Gerald first.*

"Hello!" answered Gerald's sister.

"May I speak with Gerald?" asked Mike.

"I will get him. Hold on Mike," said Gerald's sister.

"Hello," said Gerald.

"You called?" asked Mike.

"Yes, I heard the lifeguard is sending a report to our parents. It usually takes about one week. It is the pool's policy to report all incidents to all authorities and parents. You will be gone on vacation. Your parents will find out. I know you don't want them to know. But this might be a good way for them to find out, and then it would not be considered snitching." stated Gerald.

"Oh really? I hope it comes while I am on vacation," replied Mike. "That is great they are sending out the incident report. Wow! Thanks for telling me."

"It's all good. You are my buddy, and I just wanted to give you a heads-up," responded Gerald.

"Okay, partner. I am going to pack. Man, I am getting excited about my vacation," said Michael. *I had better hurry because time is passing by. It's vacation time. I forgot I need to call some of my other friends. I will after I finish packing and getting ready. Boy it's already six o'clock.*

"Veronica, I called Gerald. Who else called? It's time for dinner? What are we having tonight?" asked Michael.

"Mom bought some chicken and some vegetables for us to eat. She is doing some shopping for the trip and Dad is working late. Reggie, Abdul, Ellen and Juanita were the other ones that called," responded Veronica.

"Thanks, Sis. I had better eat before I faint. Have you finished packing?" asked Michael. "I am almost finished. I need to wash a few things. Where did Mom get this chicken? It is so good."

"The deli down the street. Aren't you going to call your friends? What is going on? All of them called about the same time? Is everything okay, Mike?" asked Veronica.

"Oh, they want to know how my summer is going, and a couple of them know we are going on vacation. They want to go with us." responded Michael. *The food was good, and I am full. I will call a couple of my friend's right after I do some more packing. I have to make sure I take a beach towel, some tennis shoes, flip-flops, shorts, deodorant,*

38

toothpaste, and lotion. I need to call my buddies. It's almost eight o'clock.

"May I speak with Reggie? "asked Mike. "This is Reggie." stated Reggie.

"Hey, Reggie, I am returning your call," said Michael.

"What's up?"

"Mike, I was just making sure you are okay. I haven't been to the pool in a while, but I heard what that Billy boy did. Are you okay?" said Reggie.

"I'm okay. I have decided not to go back to the swimming pool. That guy is a bully," stated Michael.

"I'm glad you are okay. Abdul and I had an encounter with him earlier this summer. We stopped going to the swimming pool because of him. We could tell he was a bully. We made the decision quickly to avoid him," said Reggie.

"Thanks for sharing and for your concern. I have not decided what I am going to do. I know the lifeguard is sending a copy of the incident report to the parents of the individuals involved. So maybe that will put a stop to the bullying. We are getting ready to go on vacation. I will have a lot of time to think about Billy the bully," said Mike.

"That is good. Please do something about this menace. He keeps going from one person to another, said Reggie.

"Have a safe and fun trip."

"Thanks, my friend, said Michael. I will see you after I come back from vacation. Man, if you believe in prayer, pray for me. And pray we have a safe vacation."

"I will. Have fun," said Reggie.

"Okay!" responded Michael. Now it's nine o'clock.

Veronica asked, "How are you coming on your packing? I'm almost finished. Did you call all your friends? We leave in the morning."

"No, I called a couple of them. I will have to talk to them, when I get back. Maybe I can call them, while we are traveling tomorrow," responded Mike.

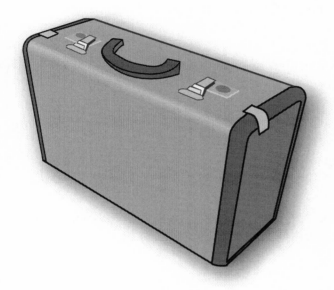

VACATION STARTS

Michael's family was up by five o'clock the next morning and ready to begin their vacation. John, Michael's father, packed the car the night before. John's sister who lives two doors down, will check on the house while her brother and his family are gone for ten days. Michael, Veronica, Mom, and Dad get in the car and take off. The children sleep for six hours of the trip.

"Who is Billy, Michael?" Veronica asks.

"What do you mean who is Billy?" asked Michael, looking startled.

"You kept calling his name in your sleep. You were telling him to stop. It seemed like you were dreaming about a real person. Don't lie to me, Michael! Who is Billy?" inquired Veronica.

"Michael played it off by saying, "I was just dreaming. It was nothing. Can't I dream in peace?" said Michael in a joking way.

"It sure seemed like a real person you were dreaming about because you kept going on and on, and you even started throwing your hands in the air as if you were fighting Billy," Veronica said with concern.

"Veronica, you are tripping girl. You act like a person cannot dream. Leave me alone," complained Michael.

Michael realized his sister is concerned, and quickly changed the subject. "Dad are we almost there?" asked Michael.

"Yes, we are twenty minutes from the hotel where we will be staying," said Dad.

"I am so excited," said Michael. "We're going to have some fun! I'm going to ride some rides, especially the roller coasters! Sister, I know you are riding with me!" screamed Michael.

"You know it," said Veronica.

Hotel Encounter

The family arrived at the hotel around one in the afternoon. That is just enough time to go one to of the theme parks at Disney World.

"Are we going to a park today?" asked Michael. His mother nodded and responded, "We are, but first we have to take a shower. We can get something to eat at the park."

Michael is excited, and said, "Boy, I am ready. I should have brought one of my friends with me to ride the rides. I wonder how they are handling Billy?"

Veronica heard Michael say Billy again and asked, "What did you say? I thought I heard you say the name Billy."

Michael smiled and lied, "No, Veronica, you did not hear me say that. You are hearing things. Let it rest."

"Children, go ahead and take your showers," said Dad. "Let's be ready in about thirty minutes. Then we can visit our first park."

In their room, Veronica confronted Michael and said she knows that he is hiding something. She cautioned Michael that she won't stop nagging him until he tells her.

In the other room, their parents are discussing Michael.

"Did you hear the conversation the children were having in the backseat? I played like I was sleep, but I heard everything," said Mom. "Knowing Veronica, she is not going to let her brother rest until he tells her what happened. I know it has something to do with the new kid on the block—his name is Billy. Michael thinks we do not know anything, but the parents in the neighborhood are talking about this new kid."

"Wow, God is answering our prayers. We cannot force Michael to tell us what is going on, but it seems to be coming to light. I know we cannot be everywhere our children are, and God is showing us he is faithful. He is protecting us and our children. I just praise God because he is watching over them. Let's just keep praying. It looks like God is using Veronica to bring out the truth," said their father.

"Oh, I wish I could watch over my baby every step of the way. But we are not Jesus, and Michael is going to be in the sixth grade. He is growing up and even children have growing pains, trials, and tribulations. It is so hard for me to see Michael suffer as he does. He thinks he is so grown up— too big for my hugs. He will always be my baby," replied their mother.

"I know you want him to be your baby forever, but he will be a man sooner than we think. We have to allow him to go through whatever God is taking him through. If someone is causing him harm, we will have to step in. But if it is just a silly argument with this Billy child, we cannot interfere with arguments. We should minister the word of God. He will resent us if we interfere with everything." stated the father.

A knock is at the door heralds the arrival of Michael and Veronica.

"Mom! Dad! We are ready!" yelled the children.

"Okay, give us a few minutes. Watch something on TV while we finish getting ready," said Mom.

Veronica and Michael sat in front of the TV and found one of their favorite shows. The topic of the show was bullying. Michael immediately turned to another channel.

"Michael, what is wrong with you? That is our favorite TV show. We never miss an episode." yelled Veronica.

"Nothing is wrong. I just don't want to watch that!" Michael responded. Let's watch something new."

"You have never had a problem with this show before. What is wrong Michael? When you were dreaming you said something about bullying—has something happened? Is someone bullying you? That episode reminds you of Billy, doesn't it? Has this Billy boy been bullying you? Is that what has been going on? Is that why you are dreaming about Billy?" asked Veronica.

"Nothing is wrong," Michael shouted. "I just want to watch something different!"

"I don't care what you say—something is going on!" hollered Veronica.

"What is going on?" said their parents in unison. What are you fighting about?"

"Nothing!" shouted Michael. "We are just fighting over what show to watch," said Veronica.

"Turn the TV off, and let's go to the park," said Dad.

The family left the hotel room, with Veronica and Michael glaring at each other. Veronica loves her brother and wants him to tell the truth. Michael knows she loves him, but he is embarrassed by the whole bullying thing.

Park Time

On the way to the park, Veronica and Michael discussed what they should ride first.

"Mom and Dad, what are you going to do while we stand in line to ride the rides?" asked Veronica.

"We will probably go to a show and then after the show stand at the exit of the ride you two are on," said Dad.

They arrive safely and proceed to the gate. Dad gives the tickets to the gate attendant. Veronica and Michael run to get in line for their favorite roller coaster. They will have to wait an hour in line.

"Michael, what is going on?" asked Veronica. "Who is bullying you?"

"Veronica, you have to promise you will not tell our parents. I see that you are not going to stop asking until I tell you." stated Michael.

"I promise I will not tell!" said Veronica. *Veronica knows in her heart of hearts that whatever is going on, if it's serious enough, she will tell her parents if it is life threatening, but she cannot tell Michael that. Veronica listens intently as Michael explains about Billy.*

"Veronica, I am confused—I don't know what I have done to Billy to deserve this treatment. Every time he has bothered me, Gerald was with me, but Billy never bothered him." stated Michael as he thinks about his problem.

"Wow, Michael, why you did not tell anyone? You could have been hurt? I am sorry that this guy has been picking on you all summer. You are a little soldier. I know you are afraid of Billy, Michael, but don't be scared of him.

48

Honestly, Michael, this bullying has reached the point that you need to include authority figures. I am not going to tell our parents right now. But I will be on the lookout when we get back. If something else happens, I am telling Mom and Dad. Listen brother, you have done nothing wrong. Bullies are miserable people, and I guarantee that something is going on in his life, and he wants to take it out on you." responded Veronica.

"Please do not tell! I am not going to die. I can handle it myself, Sis, I thought I could trust you." said Michael with concern in his voice.

"You can trust me!" Veronica replied. "I was not going to tell, but if your life is in danger from here on out, I have an obligation to say something. I am not going to live without my only sibling. I would not be able to live with myself. I would expect you to do the same for me."

"I know I should have said something. I think I was feeling guilty. During Vacation Bible School, I gained some understanding. And what you just said helps me understand. It's like he is hurting, and he wants me to hurt. I don't know what is going on with him. One scripture that is helping me is Love your enemies. I learned it in Vacation Bible School.

Billy is my enemy. God wants me to forgive him. He has to be responsible for his actions. Thanks, sis!" said Michael.

"You are welcome, Brother," said Veronica, as she gave him a hug. "Now, let's enjoy our vacation."

Vacation Is Over

The vacation was very relaxing and enjoyable for Michael and Veronica. Their parents also had an awesome time. It was a well-needed vacation for all four of them. They made it back to their hometown safely. It was a Sunday afternoon, and school would start a week from tomorrow. Michael was particularly excited because he knew he and Billy were not going to the same school.

On the Monday and Tuesday of the week before school, their mother took both Veronica and Michael shopping for school clothes and supplies. On Wednesday, both children had their hair cut. The next day is orientation at their schools.

Michael entered the school and saw his friends at the orientation session. As soon as the session ended, Billy passes by and gave them an evil look.

"What in the world is he doing here?" Gerald said.

"Oh my God! He cannot be in the sixth or seventh grade! He looks like a giant that belongs in the ninth or tenth grade! Oh my God, what am I going to do, if he bothers me? My sister has threatened to tell my parents if he bothers me again." exclaimed Michael.

"Well, someone needs to tell someone. You could have died when he threw you in the swimming pool," Gerald said.

"What I am going to do? I am tired of that big bully picking on me. Something has got to be done, but I am scared. I am so disappointed that he is going to our school," said Michael.

The boys left the school and walked home. Both Michael and Gerald are brainstorming to figure out how to handle Billy. They were thrown for a loop when they saw Billy at their school. They decided that it is time for something to be done. They know Billy is not going to leave Michael alone.

Michael, Gerald, Veronica, and their friends spend the next few days getting ready for school. Michael and Gerald have mixed emotions about the first day of school.

51

First Day of School

The first day of school has finally arrived. Michael has butterflies in his stomach as he enters the school; he was running late on the first day of school.

The day runs smoothly during the first, second, third, and fourth periods. Fifth period is Michael's gym class, and he runs into Billy. Billy grabs him by his shirt. Michael tries to push Billy away from him. It's a struggle. Billy is persistent. The struggle goes on for a few minutes.

Billy began speaking. "I'll be back for more." Billy walked away.

Boy am I relieved. Michael thought to himself. He finally went away.

Michael is scared, and he wish Billy would just leave him alone. Michael knows in his heart he must do something.

The first four days of school went smoothly. Michael didn't have any close encounters with Billy. That soon changed.

Billy Starts Again

Billy was back to his old tactics and Michael was his
favorite target. He does his dirty work in front of people.
Again, Michael did not say anything, but the fear and stress
caused him to yell at his friends and family. Michael should
channel this anger toward Billy. Billy was angry at his
family for not showing him love, and Michael was angry at
Billy. They were taking their anger out on the wrong person.

Billy ran by Michael's locker and slammed the door closed. It was becoming too much for Michael to handle. Michael started praying and asking God to help him. Michael cried and cried out to God. Then after he cried and prayed Michael began thanking God every day and all throughout the day. He decided to trust God like he had seen his parents do.

The following Monday, Billy pushed Michael down as they entered the basketball court. He had glanced in the coach's office, and no one was there. There were a few students in the locker room.

Billy saw this as the perfect time to bother Michael. But there is a God, the coach saw Billy push Michael.

"You come here!" said the coach, signaling for Billy to stand before him. "Why did you push him?"

"I did not push him," Billy lied.

The coach responded with disgust, "You did! I was right behind you when you pushed him. Don't let me see you push him again. We do not tolerate that type of behavior at our school. If it happens again, you will be suspended! Now go out there and play some basketball." Billy just looked at the coach but did not respond. Billy didn't think the coach was serious.

Billy hates Michael; he is jealous. Michael has the clothes, the family, and the love. His dislike for Michael is growing. He constantly plots what he can do to aggravate him. He keeps bothering Michael because nothing has been done to stop him. Billy will continue bothering Michael until he is stopped.

55

Can You Believe it

"Mike, I cannot believe Billy is in your gym class and goes to our school," said Gerald, as he and Michael ate lunch together.

"God is faithful. I have been praying and thanking God for helping me get Billy off my back. I have not done anything to him." Anger is building up in Michael as he speaks. "It is really getting on my nerves. I am trusting in God. But it is hard. I have never been through anything like this. One good thing has occurred—the coach saw him push me and told him not to do it again or he will get suspended. Billy did not look scared—in fact, he looked like he didn't care," replied Michael.

"That is great, Michael. The coach saw him, maybe something will be done soon. I am tired of it, too. I don't know what to do, and sometimes I feel like I am failing you as your buddy. I just get still and act like a zombie. In my heart of hearts, I want to help you my friend, but I just freeze I think if you were in my shoes you would do more than what I have done Michael." said Gerald.

I must admit that I have been scared and honestly did not know what to do. My sister forced me to tell her. She kept asking me until I told her me while we were on family vacation. To tell the truth, I am glad she pulled it out of me," stated Michael with a sigh of relief.

The school day ends, and everyone goes home. Michael does his homework as soon as he gets home. He desired to keep his straight A's. Billy is thinking to himself. I'm going to beat Michael as much as I can. I don't care if I get in trouble. I don't like Michael and his friends. Since Michael is so afraid of me, I'll keep bullying him.

Veronica's Interrogation

It's before dinnertime. Michael is doing his homework. Veronica knocks at his door.

"Come on in, Sis," said Michael.

"Hello, Brother, how has the new school year been going? Do you like your classes?" asked Veronica.

"So far, my classes are great, and I like my teachers. I have a heavy load, I am taking pre-algebra this year. So far, I am making an A," said Michael.

"What school does Billy attend?" asked Veronica. Michael paused. "He attends my school, and he is in my gym class.

58

He is getting on my nerves, Veronica. I just want to slap him, but I know God would not be pleased. I want to punch him in the stomach. He's a lot bigger, so I'm afraid that if I retaliate, he'd quickly overpower me."

"I hear you, Michael. You are nicer than me—I would have hit him by now," claimed Veronica.

"I have made up my mind that I will do what I need to do to get this problem solved. I have asked God to help me. I am thanking God for helping me too," declared Michael.

"I am glad to hear that, brother. I know you do not want me to step in. I thank God you are trusting him, and willing to do your part as he leads you," said Veronica.

"No, I do not want you to handle it. The talk at the school and in the neighborhood will be Michael's sister had to handle the bully, Billy. No that would be too embarrassing," said Michael.

"You know I will step in to handle Billy, if it comes to that. He needs to pick on someone his own size. I know that would be embarrassing for you, so I will try not to intervene. I will see you at dinner, brother. I love you, even though you get on my nerves at times. If something was to happen to you, I do not know what I would do," said Veronica in a loving way.

"I love you, too, and you get on my nerves, too." said Michael, smiling. "See you at dinner."

"Later!" said Veronica.

We Are Family

One and a half hours later, it's dinnertime, and Mom calls the family to the table. Everyone arrives at the table.

"Veronica, please say grace," asks Dad.

"Dear Lord, thank you for the food we are about to receive and let it be nourishment to our body. And Lord we thank you for providing our family its daily needs and watching over us. It is in Jesus name. Amen." said Veronica.

"Amen!" said the others. Everyone starts eating. There is silence.

"Honey, this meal you put together is delicious. I am so glad God sent you to me. You make my life easy. You are a virtuous woman," said their father.

"Oh, Mom and Dad, cut the mushy stuff out!" said Michael.

"I think it is beautiful that you still appreciate each other after twenty years of marriage. One day, I want a husband just like you, Dad. You treat mother like a queen," said Veronica.

"Thank you, Princess. It is our prayer that you will marry a gentleman who treats you right," said Dad.

"You are a great example, Dad!" said Veronica.

"Thanks, honey! It makes me feel good that you notice how I treat your mother. My prayer is that the way I treat your mother will be an example of what you should receive when you decide to get married," responded Dad.

"How is school going for the both of you?" asked Dad.

"School is going fine. Things are working out and unfolding in every area of my life. I have no complaints, father." said Michael.

"Are you sure, honey?" said Mom.

61

"Yes, Mother, everything is going fine. Please do not worry about me. I am handling everything. God is working it out. Thanks Mom and Dad for teaching me about God and his son Jesus. I am discovering God is faithful," stated Michael.

"I am glad God is working it out!" responded mom gratefully.

"Yes, Mother," said Michael. "Remember what you taught me—the angels of the Lord are encamped about me. God has sent his angels to protect me always. I am a living witness that God watches over you. "I am glad he watches over us! I am glad everything is working out for you," sighed Mom, the relief apparent in her voice.

"I am, too!" replied Dad, with a smile on his face.

"Me, too!" stated Veronica with excitement in her voice.

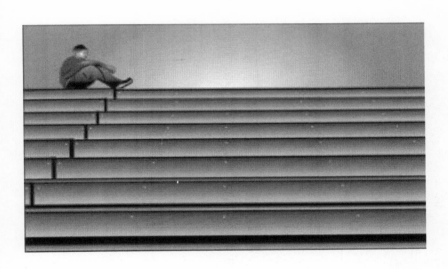

The Saga Continues

The next day at school Michael's classes went along smoothly. He is full of excitement and joy because he knows

God is watching over him. Michael goes to his gym class and changes into his gym clothes. The coach has the students sit on the bleachers. Everyone starts climbing the bleachers and they hear a loud thump.

Billy pushed Michael down while climbing the bleachers.

"Oh my God," one student said.

"Oh, no," another student said.

"Billy, I saw you push him. Go to the principal's office. I will join you there in a minute." said the disgusted and angry coach.

Billy did not respond. He was surprised and shocked that the coach saw him push Michael down. He wondered what the consequences would be for pushing Michael down.

"Go to the principal's office. Why am I repeating myself? I will be there in a minute," yelled the coach.

"Are you okay," asked the assistant coach with much concern. It looks like your arm is broken. I hope that is all. I think we should take you to the hospital."

The assistant coach decided to take Michael to the hospital, and he also called Michael's parents. They are nervous and praying that it is not too serious. The coach had to stop by the principal's office before leaving.

"Billy, you are new to this school, and you are starting out wrong. You should make friends not enemies. Why did you do it? We have zero tolerance for this type of behavior," said the principal.

64

"Hello, Coach. Thanks for coming. I am going to suspend Billy for one week. When he comes back he will be required to go to counseling sessions twice a week," said the principal. "Coach, do you think this punishment is severe enough?"

"It should probably be two weeks. That will give him plenty of time to have regrets. He will need to attend counseling sessions until he is released. I have seen him bothering Michael since school started. I ignored the first couple of incidents, and I warned him not to do it again. I guess he did not take my warnings seriously," said the coach.

"I have a question for Billy. Do you realize the seriousness of this incident?" asked the principal.

"No, I was just playing! said Billy.

"You shouldn't play like that. You're acting like a bully, said the principal. "We will need your parents to attend some counseling sessions with you. The part that really bothers me is you did it again after the coach told you not to. You disregarded the coach's instructions and authority."

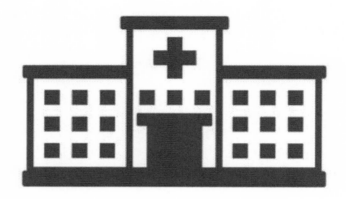

At the Hospital

Michael's mother dashes up to the nurse's station in the emergency room. "Can you tell me where Michael Jones is?" she asks with concern.

"He is in the x-ray room. I believe they are almost finished," replied the nurse.

At that moment, Michael's father entered the emergency room.

"Honey, is Michael okay? Where is he?" asked the father.

"He is in x-ray. They are almost finished, so we should see him soon," said Mom.

Michael approaches with a nurse, and his parents rush toward him.

"How are you?" mom asked.

"I am fine, Mother. I am still alive." said Michael with excitement in his voice.

"What happened? Did Billy do this?" asked Dad. Michael looked surprised, his dad continued, "We don't know all the details. We have bits and pieces of the story."

"I hope he has been punished for doing this to you," stated Mom angrily.

"I am going to the school tomorrow!" said Dad.

"I am coming with you! Both of us showing up will let them know there is no tolerance of this type of behavior!" responded Mrs. Jones with concern.

A doctor approached the family and asks, "Are you the parents?"

"Yes, we are," said Michael's parents.

"Does he have any broken bones?" inquired Mom. "He only has a broken arm. That is a miracle. He does not have to miss any school because it is his left arm, and Michael told me he is right-handed," said the doctor.

"Are you going to prescribe something for pain?" asked Mrs. Jones.

67

"Yes, here is the prescription. It will help with the swelling and pain," said the doctor.

"Thanks! We appreciate how you have taken care of our son," stated Mrs. Jones with a smile.

"You are welcome. I want to see Michael for a follow-up visit to my office within the next three weeks," instructed the doctor.

"We'll be there. Thanks again," Mr. Jones said.

"You're welcome," said the doctor.

The family left the hospital relieved and grateful to God.

The Principal's Office

The next morning, Michael's parents presented themselves at the principal's office.

"Good morning! We are Mr. and Mrs. Jones, Michael's parents. Our son has a broken arm, and we want to know exactly what happened in the gym yesterday. We understand from our son that he was pushed by a classmate named Billy. We want to know what is being done with Billy," said Mr. Jones, Michael's father.

"I am sorry to hear that Michael has a broken arm," said the school secretary. "He is a good student. I will call the principal and see if the coach can come down also."

She calls the principal and the coach. The parents take a seat to wait. In a few minutes, the principal enters the room.

"Good morning, Mr. and Mrs. Jones. I am Mr. Bernard, the principal. I am truly sorry that Michael has had this experience with Billy. Please step into my office and have a seat. The coach is on his way to meet with us. I want to assure you that we have done everything possible to handle this situation," stated the principal.

The office door opened, and the coach entered the room, nodding at the Joneses, Michael's parents, and the principal.

"Good morning," said the coach.

"I was just informing Mr. and Mrs. Jones that we have started working on the punishment for Billy. We have suspended him for two weeks and he will be required to take counseling classes for several weeks. We plan to include his parents in the counseling sessions. We have informed him that if an incident likes this happens again, he will be expelled from this school. He would have to go to an alternative school," explained the principal.

"Yes, Mr. and Mrs. Jones, unfortunately, Billy pushed your son down the bleachers. I want to apologize to you for what your family is experiencing," said the coach.

"We have contacted Billy's parents, so far they have not called us back," said the principal.

"I am glad you are handling this situation. We knew something was going on. We asked Michael several times, but he would not tell us. Thank God he finally shared the problem with his sister during our vacation two weeks ago. This young man has been bothering Michael all summer. And from my understanding he has been bothering other children." said Mr. Jones.

"Thanks again for everything. I would like to follow up on Billy's status, if possible. He must be a miserable child to go around beating up on children." said Mrs. Jones, Michael's mom.

"You can inquire, but there is only so much information I can give you. We can give you a synopsis of what the counselor says," said the principal.

"Thanks again for taking care of my son and Billy," said Mr. Jones.

"We will be in touch," said Mrs. Jones.

The Interview at Dinnertime

It's dinnertime and the Jones family is gathered around the table.

"Thank you for the food we are about to receive, we ask that this food be of nourishment to our bodies, in Jesus name. We thank you also, Father, for answering our prayers, in Jesus name," said Dad.

"Amen!" said Michael. "I am starving."

"Me too!" said Veronica.

"Mom, this food is good." said Michael.

"I agree," said Veronica.

"How was everyone's day?" asked Mom. "Michael, we will start with you. We asked you repeatedly what was going on with you this summer. You refused to tell us, and we let you slide. We knew you were lying to us. We knew that God would reveal it all. We deliberately asked you on more than one occasion if everything was okay with you. You constantly said no.

God started revealing everything to us, little by little. First, he had some neighbors tell us that Billy was bullying the children in the neighborhood, including you. We watched you every day, and we could tell when you had trouble with Billy. You would come home and be very reserved. You would bestand offish, and short with your answers. God is faithful," said Dad.

"Michael, your father is saying that it does not pay to lie to us. First, it is wrong. Because we serve God and love God, he is not going to let any hurt or harm come to our children. I thank God for you all. I am glad God is watching over you," said Mom.

"I am so sorry! Please forgive me Mom, Dad, and Veronica. I thought I could handle it on my own. I did not want to include you. And to be truthful, I was embarrassed and ashamed. Little did I know that bullies have been around forever. I did not realize they are miserable within themselves. Please forgive me. That was the worst thing I have ever been through in my life. God is faithful, and I guess I was trying to be God. What a lesson to learn. I am glad the school officials are involved now. I do have more peace now," said Michael in a relieved and grateful way.

"It could have been worse. I thank God for watching over you." said Mom.

"Wow, there is nothing for me to say, but thank God! Yes, God is faithful," said Dad.

<u>Counseling Time</u>

"Billy how are you doing, today?" asked the counselor.

"I am okay," replied Billy.

"Will your mother and father be able to make it today?" asked the counselor.

"I'm not sure," responded Billy.

"I guess we can get started. I will give them a call after our session is over. After reading your chart I understand you are here because you had a confrontation with a student by the name of Michael. Do you want to tell me about it?" asked the counselor.

No, not really," said Billy.

"Billy, I know you might not want to talk about it, but unfortunately, if we do not begin somewhere you will prolong your counseling sessions. It will be up to me to decide if you need to stop coming to counseling," said the counselor. "I'll tell you what let's start off with something else. How was your summer?"

"It was okay," Billy responds with obvious irritation.

"From my understanding, you moved here from Houston. Is that correct?" asked the counselor.

"Yes," said Billy.

"Billy maybe you should come back another day. You are not very responsive today. Would you like to leave?" asked the counselor.

"Good-bye." said Billy."

The counselor calls Billy's parents but no one answers.

The counselor leaves a message on his mom's cell. Hello, this is Billy's counselor at the school. Please give me a call at 004-425-9877."

The counselor then called the father. His dad answered.

"This is Billy's counselor from school. I was expecting you to show up for our counseling session today," said the counselor.

"I was not able to make it, as a matter of fact I will be traveling a lot during the next six weeks, so I will not be able to make any of the sessions," said his dad.

"Oh, I see. I am sorry to hear that. And there is no way you can change your schedule?" asked the counselor.

"No, I cannot. The job is really strict about our schedule. I would suggest that you call my wife. She should be able to make it." said Billy's father.

"I left a message on your wife's phone. I am sorry that you can't participate. Thanks, maybe you can follow-up by telephone.

"Maybe I can."

"Great! Call me once a week to see how the sessions are coming along. Thanks. Good-bye!" said the counselor.

"I will. Good-bye."

Billy's Home Life

Billy went home; he really wanted to be mean to the counselor, but he knew that would prolong his counseling sessions. He decided he would talk more at the next session. By this time, Billy was mad at the world. He was mad at his parents, Michael, the counselor, and anyone who got in his way.

Life at Billy's house does not exemplify the best place of love, and Billy needs love and attention.

"Hello, Mom!" said Billy.

"Hello, Billy. Dinner is ready. You can eat whenever you want. I just got messages off my phone from your principal and your counselor. They want me to come to the school. I hope you have been behaving Billy. I do not have time to take off from work." said his mom.

"I had a fight, Mother that is all," said Billy.

Did you start the fight?" asked his mom.

"Yes," replied Billy.

"What happened?" inquired his mom.

"I hit this boy named Michael. He stepped on my toes," lied Billy.

"I hope you are telling me the truth. That is an automatic one-week punishment. You will stay in the house for one week. I am taking the cell phone, TV, and computer from you. I told you when we moved here from Houston there would be no more fighting. You have started fighting, and it is only the first week of school," said his mom.

"Oh, Mom! I could not help it! I was caught off guard," explained Billy.

"No excuses! I told you the bullying would have to stop when we were moved here from Houston. You cannot bring the problems you had in Houston here. You have not changed.   Do you remember that conversation your father and I had with you? You cannot continue to bully people. We don't have time for this." stated mom.

"I vaguely remember the conversation," stated Billy.

"You have selective memory. Now I must go up to your school in the next morning," stated Billy's mom.

Billy's Mother Goes to the School

The next morning, Billy's mother went to the school She is not happy because she loses money when she takes off work.

"Good morning, I am here to see the principal. I am the mother of Billy Williams," said his mom.

"Good morning, Mrs. Williams. I am glad you were able to get off work to come see me. Working two jobs must be hard on you," inquired the principal.

"I just found out about Billy's fight last night. Billy told me he hit this boy named Michael. I have put him on punishment for a week," stated his mom.

"Billy did not give you all the information. He has been picking on Michael all summer. Unfortunately, it carried over to the school year. He was warned by our coach not to bother Michael again. The last time he bothered Michael, he pushed Michael down, and Michael broke his arm. We suspended Billy for two weeks, and he is attending counseling sessions until the counselor releases him. We are expecting you and your husband to attend the counseling sessions with Billy," said the principal.

"I had no idea this was going on. Can you call Billy into the office? I cannot believe this started this summer. I am working hard trying to make ends meet. I guess I have failed as a parent," said Billy's mother.

"You have not failed as a parent. It's just that you have so much to concentrate on. I am quite sure you love and care for Billy. That is why you work so hard," said the principal.

The coach and Billy enter the principal's office and took seats.

"Good morning Billy," said the principal.

"Good morning," said Billy, glancing at his mom.

"Good morning, Billy. I have learned that you have not been telling me the truth. And why not?" asked his mom.

"I did not think you cared," responded Billy.

"Billy, I care! That is why I work so hard to make ends meet and to provide for you. I do all of this because I love you. I admit I do not spend enough time with you. Please forgive me! Your father also cares!" explained the mother.

"I forgive you! I don't believe Daddy cares," said Billy.

"He does. He does not know how to say it or show it. It seems like I can improve in that area, too," stated mom.

"Thanks, Mom!" said Billy. He and his mother hug.

"Thanks for coming in, Mrs. Williams. I hope you can make it to several of Billy's counseling sessions," said the principal.

"I will try." replied the mother.

Counseling Time Again

"Hello!" said the counselor. "This is our second session, and I hope you're ready."

"Hello," said Billy.

"How are you today?" asked the counselor.

"I'm doing okay," said Billy.

"Your mother came to the school today. How was that? Do you think your mother will make it in?" inquired the counselor.

"It was okay. I don't think she will be in this evening. She cannot take off work anymore. My father definitely will not be here," said Billy.

"Why do you say that, Billy?" asked the counselor.

"Even though my father lives in our house. It's a miracle if I see him once a month. My mother finally took some time out to see what is going on in my life. She is always working." stated Billy.

Billy, your mother must work to provide for you. She does love you. She might have to learn how to show it to you. We will have to convey to your parents that you need attention," said the counselor.

"You call that love! It is like my parents don't exist! I see my mother twice a week and my father once a month!" yelled Billy angrily.

"Billy, please do not feel that way. There is love in your family. I did talk to your mother and your father. Some people have a strange way of showing it," replied the counselor.

"I have no one to talk to! My father is not available! We played sports together before we moved here! We talked about my dreams! My mom and I were closer! It's like they do not exist!" said Billy.

"So are you angry and mad at your parents. You are taking your anger out on Michael. You have what we call displaced anger. You need love. You are mad because you think you are not receiving it," stated the counselor.

"Maybe I am!" replied Billy. "Life is not fair! My daddy is so busy. He does not have time for me. My mom neither."

"Yes, Billy, sometimes life can throw some hard blows. I apologize that you have not had anyone to talk to," said the counselor.

Billy responds by saying, "Thanks, Can I leave now?"

"One thing before you leave—I want you to know that even though your parents are not always available, it does not mean you can mistreat others. You are accountable for your own actions. I believe we have made progress today. See you in a couple of days. For our next session, I want you to think about why you bully Michael. Are you jealous? From my records, I see that you live a few houses from him. So, you get to see Michael at school, at home, and play." said the counselor.

"I will think on that. I do feel better now that I opened up to you. Good-bye!" said Billy.

<u>Billy is being a Bully</u>

That evening, Billy sees Michael spending time with his
father. It looked like they're having a good conversation

from a distance. Billy starts to envy Michael and his relationship with his father. Billy tells himself he should not be envious. But then he turns around and sees James, another classmate, playing sports with his father. Hopefully, Billy continues to get healed and not allow envy and jealousy to overrule him.

The next day at school during the fifth grade a couple of weeks after Billy returned from school after he was suspended. You wonder if he learned anything from being suspended. Billy sees James and wants to bother him. There are children in the hallway watching Billy, they know he is up to something. Billy pushed him several times. After the third time, James does a karate move on Billy and brings him to his knees. Everyone standing around applauded. Billy was humiliated and ran off. Please note that James is four feet-ten inches. Billy is rather tall. Billy thought he could push James around.

Billy skipped the rest of the school day. He was surprised and amazed that James was able bring him down. This incident was the talk of the school. Billy was embarrassed.

During the sixth period of school, everyone was talking about it.

Abdul asked, "Did you hear what happened to Billy?"

"Yes, that karate-kicking James took him down!" yelled a classmate with excitement.

In another classroom, Juanita asked her classmate,

"Did you hear that the bully Billy got knocked down by little James? He asked for that!"

"Girl, yes I heard. Yes, he had it coming to him," replied another classmate.

In another classroom, Ellen asked, "Did you hear what happened to Billy? I am sorry it happened to him, but he truly asked for it. He just moved in the community this past summer, and he has been bullying all of my neighbors, including me."

In yet another classroom, "Man did you hear about what happened to Billy? He got his butt kicked," stated John.

The school bell rang for the end of the day. All the children went home. The talk of the school is that Billy was pushed down by James. It's like in the Bible when David defeated the giant Goliath.

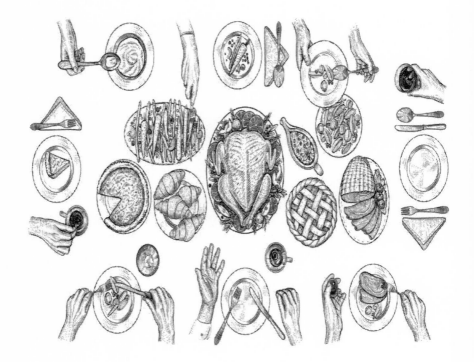

Family Time

"How was school today Veronica?" asked her father.

"My day was great, Dad! I made an A my test that I was concerned about." said Veronica.

Dad and mother replied, "That was great!"

"Awesome! I am glad to know you are applying yourself and doing your part to make a good grade," said Mom.

"God is good!" said Daddy. "I am so proud of you."

"Thanks, Mom and Dad," said Veronica. "Thanks for always praying for me and supporting me."

"You are welcome, honey," said Mom.

"How was your day, Michael?" asked Daddy.

"My day was great! Something interesting happened. You know the scripture says about do unto others as you would have them do unto you, and the other one, you shall reap what you sow? Wow I saw God's word operating today," said Michael.

"What happened?" asked Daddy.

"Billy started picking on James today. James allowed him to push him two times before he responded. James gave Billy a karate kick, and Billy fell to the floor. After a few seconds on the floor, he got up and ran out of the building. You must see the real picture—Billy is almost six feet and James is not even five feet. It was like David and Goliath. Billy thought James could not defend himself." said Michael.

"Wow!" said Veronica.

"God is awesome!" said Mom.

"God's laws do not lie," said Dad. "I am quite sure James caught him by surprise. You are right Michael, you do reap what you sow. God's laws do not lie. We must keep praying for Billy."

91

"Yes, Dad, I pray for him. It is a good feeling when you do not hold a grudge against someone. God is good," said Michael.

"Yes, honey, it is good you pray for Billy. I can imagine what Billy is thinking. God bless him!" said Mom.

"Yes!" said Veronica.

"I am amazed at the awesomeness of God," said Michael.

"That is great that you have been able to maintain your grades after all you have been through. I am proud of you!" said mom.

"Yes, that is great, Michael! I am proud of you. Keep up the good work!" said Daddy.

"Veronica and Michael, you know we love you," said Mom.

"And we love you and Dad!" said Veronica.

"Yes, mother," said Michael. "Can we eat now?"

"Of course!" said Mom. "Let's eat!"

Billy in the Principal's Office Again

The next morning at school, James and Billy are called into the principal's office.

"Good morning, James. Step into my office. Have a seat," said the principal.

"Okay," replied James.

"Would you like to tell me what happened yesterday afternoon?" asked the principal.

"Well, Billy pushed me twice. The third time, I gave him a karate kick, and he fell to the floor. After he had been on the floor for a few seconds, he ran out of the school building," explained James.

" I cannot fault you for protecting yourself. You know we do not condone fighting. I will give you some   grace and not suspend you. We have never had any problems from you. Students pick on you, but you restrain and resist. Do not begin to make your karate kicks a habit," said the principal.

In the hallway, before Billy made it to the principal's office, he ran into the coach.

"Billy!" yelled the coach.

Billy slowed down and looked at the coach.

"Billy you skipped my class yesterday. I heard what happened, and I hate to say it, but you reaped what you sowed. You cannot push people thinking no one is going to retaliate. I know you are embarrassed that a short guy like James knocked you down. Hopefully, you will consider not bullying people anymore since James knocked you down," said the coach.

"I hear you, Coach and understand." responded Billy.

Billy continued to the principal's office and had a seat outside. He is a little nervous.

"Billy, I know you know why you are in my office this morning. Tell me what happened yesterday right before your gym class started," asked the principal.

"I was knocked down by James! He used one of his karate moves on me!" replied Billy.

94

"Are you saying James performed his karate on you first?" asked the principal.

"No." replied Billy.

"How did the fight begin?" asked the principal.

"I started it," stated Billy as he hung his head down and responded as if he was whispering.

"Speak up!" said the principal.

"I started it," said Billy.

"Tell me what happened!" demanded the principal.

"I pushed him," said Billy.

"How many times did you push him?" asked the principal.

"I pushed him three times. After that he karate kicked me," said Billy.

"The third time you pushed him, James decided to retaliate!" said the principal. "Billy how does it feel to get some of your own medicine? Have you learned that bullying anyone is wrong?" asked the principal.

Billy did not answer. He was still in awe that James karate kicked him. He was rethinking his behavior.

"Did you hear what I said Billy?" asked the principal.

"It does not feel so good," replied Billy in a somber kind of way.

"I am not going to suspend you. I believe you have been humiliated enough. I know you were embarrassed when your classmates saw this incident yesterday. I heard they applauded. Remember, you have to watch how you treat people," said the principal.

"Am I free to go?" asked Billy.

"Yes, you may leave. Remember, no more bullying. One more thing, how are your counseling sessions going?" said the principal.

"The sessions are okay. I am learning to open up. They will probably be over soon. Thanks for asking. Goodbye," said Billy.

"That is great. Progress is being made. Good day to you," said the principal.

Billy left the principal's office and spent the rest of the day trying to avoid the student body. He was embarrassed. Billy skipped the second half of the school day. He hides in the old gym.

Another Counseling Session

Billy knocked on the counselor's door. He is scared to go in but knows he must. He knows the counselor has heard about the incident with James.

"Come in," said the counselor.

"Hello," said Billy.

"Have a seat. How are you this evening? asked the counselor.

"I'm okay," answers Billy. I have a lot of homework to do.

"You have had an eventful twenty-four hours per the report I received from the principal. Do you want to tell me about it?" asked the counselor.

"I had a fight with this guy named James," said Billy.

"How did it get started?" asked the counselor.

Billy paused. "I started it."

"Tell me about it," said the counselor.

"I pushed James two times. Then I pushed him a third time. The third time, James performed a karate kick on me. That knocked me down to the ground. I was shocked. I could not believe this was happening," said Billy with amazement.

"How did that make you feel?" asked the counselor.

"It made me feel bad, and I was mad! I was shocked. I could not believe someone has beaten me at my game. Please don't say it! I know I reaped what I sowed! You will be the hundredth person to tell me that in the last twenty-four hours. I am still in awe and amazement that this guy James, knocked me down. He is much smaller than me. I have learned my lesson—I HAVE REAPED WHAT I SOWED, AND I WILL NOT BE BULLYING ANYONE ELSE!" said Billy.

"Billy, I am glad to hear you say that you know you reaped what you sowed. As far as I am concerned, we do not need to meet anymore. I am proud of you! You have learned your lesson. You can admit that you were wrong. If you need to talk to me about anything, just let me know. I will follow up with you in thirty days. Your mother has made a conscious effort to spend time with you. I am glad things are better for you at home," said the counselor.

"Thanks! This was a hard twenty-four hours. It hit me like lightning. It does not feel so good to get a piece of your own medicine," stated Billy.

"Yes, getting a taste of your medicine is tough. I hope things continue to improve for you. Good-bye Billy," said the counselor. "I hope you and your neighborhood classmates will begin to be friends. You must treat them right. See you in thirty days. I believe I should do a follow up."

"I will be surprised if they forgive me. Thanks for everything," said Billy.

Within two weeks, James and Michael had started speaking to Billy. They knew they needed to forgive Billy. By the third week, James had invited Billy to have lunch with him. Michael and James knew that if Billy would treat them with respect, they could befriend him. They knew they had to forgive him regardless. And so, did the other children.

Time for the counselor's follow-up meeting.

"Good afternoon, Billy!" said the counselor.

"Hello!" replied Billy.

"I have been watching you for the past thirty days. I noticed you are being more respectful and nicer to others in the school. James and Michael have even befriended you. I am glad you are not bullying your classmates anymore. All things worked out in the end. Thank God!" stated the counselor.

"Yes, I have new friends. I am surprised they want to be my friends, after I treated them so bad. That is a miracle. I am glad I have friends. My classmates are welcoming me to the school and the neighborhood. I realized I was driving people away. I am glad James knocked me down. That incident taught me a lot. And my parents are spending time with me.

Thanks for everything," stated Billy.

WORKBOOK

1. Questions

2. Pictures to color

3. Games

4. Pictures to color

QUESTIONS

1.What is a bully?

2.Why does a person bully?

3.Describe what bullying is?

4.Have you ever been bullied before?

5.What happened when you were bullied?

6.Describe what happened.

7.Did you tell your parents?

8.If it happened at school, did you tell your teacher, counselor, or principal?

9.How long did the bullying occur before it stopped?

10.Have you witnessed someone getting bullied?

11. If yes what did you do?

12.In the beginning of the book Juanita and Ellen were bullied.

13. What would you do different if you had the same exact experience they did?

14. Do you think Michael handled his bullying situation the best way?

15. What would you do different from Michael?

16. Do you think Michael should have told his sister sooner?

17. Do you think Michael should have told his parents sooner?

18. Earlier, you answered why do people bully. In this book, can you tell me why you think Billy was a bully?

19. If you were Billy, would you have done anything different if you were new to a school and the neighborhood?

20. Name the different types of bullying.

21. How often do you see bullying in your school?

22.What do you do when you see bullying?

23.If you don't do anything when you see bullying.

24.If you were being bullied would not you want someone to speak up on your behalf?

25. Should we abide by the golden rule-do unto other as you would have them do unto you?

These children are different-
Should you bully them?

Bullying takes place all over the world-Stop the Bullying

NO BULLYING

UNSCRAMBLE THE WORDS

1. Ybllu

2. Ictvim

3. Yublling

4. Amifly

5. Add

6. Ovel

7. Chereat

8. Icprnalpi

9. Ccoah

10. Oucnesrol

11. Loscho

12. Lyamfi

FILL IN THE BLANKS

1. b_ll_ing

2. h_r_ss

3. s_l_ este_m

4. v_c_tim

5. in_lmi_at_

6. co_f_ict

7. i_n_re

8. e_cl_de

FIND WORDS FROM THE STORY-
BILLY DON'T BE A BULLY

The words go straight across. Words to find are:

1. Billy 2. Williams 3. Jones 4. Bully 5. Gerald 6. Family 7. Principal 8. Veronica 9. Dad 10. James 11. Abdul 12. Michael 13. Coach 14. Counsel 15. Counselor

```
H Y B I L L Y J K L M N O S H E T Z Y U A M A
B A C X D G O M Z X I T E F X M I C H A E L N
J P B V G R T I M P P W Q A B U L L Y M O T H
E R A L A Z J A M E S S A L L Y A V Z T R Y H
M B D Q Z X C D A D V V C O A C H U Y T R E
W Q S D Z X V E R O N I C A B B X X O P P U Y
G F S A F G N N M N B V C V B N J H G Y T R
E A B S U L Z X S W Q M F A M I L Y Z Z D S A
Y T I O P H G F D S A Z X S S D F G Y T N N C
C O U N S E L R D X Z Q A N Z P R I N C I P A L
B B D D S A I E Y T F O P Y H I H G E R A L D N
N H J H Y T R E E W J O N E S A V L H V G F E
E R R B U L L Y I N G O I Y R E W Q C O U N S
E L O R C D E R S T Y Y U V G T T E W I L L I A
M S E R U T R E S W E R T E W E R T T T E R T
E W F C O U N S E L O R J I K L M T E M S D F
T W E W I L L I A M S P P I I T O V O P E S T A
```

<u>NO BULLYING</u>

113

Answers to the Unscramble Game

1. bully 2. victim 3. bullying 4. family 5. dad 6. love 7. teacher 8. principal 9. coach 10. counselor 11. school 12. family

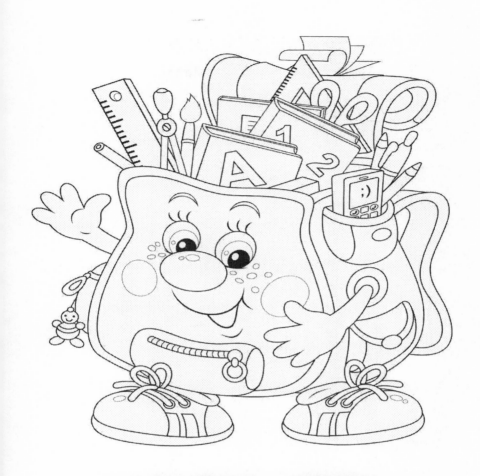

NO BULLYING AT SCHOOL

TREAT YOUR CLASSMATES
WITH RESPECT

BULLYING IS NOT NICE

ANSWERS TO THE FILL IN THE BLANK GAME

1. BULLYING
2. HARASS
3. SELF ESTEEM
4. VICTIM
5. INTIMIDATOR
6. CONFLICT
7. IGNORE
8. EXCLUDE